3)⁸/₁₀

Cottone

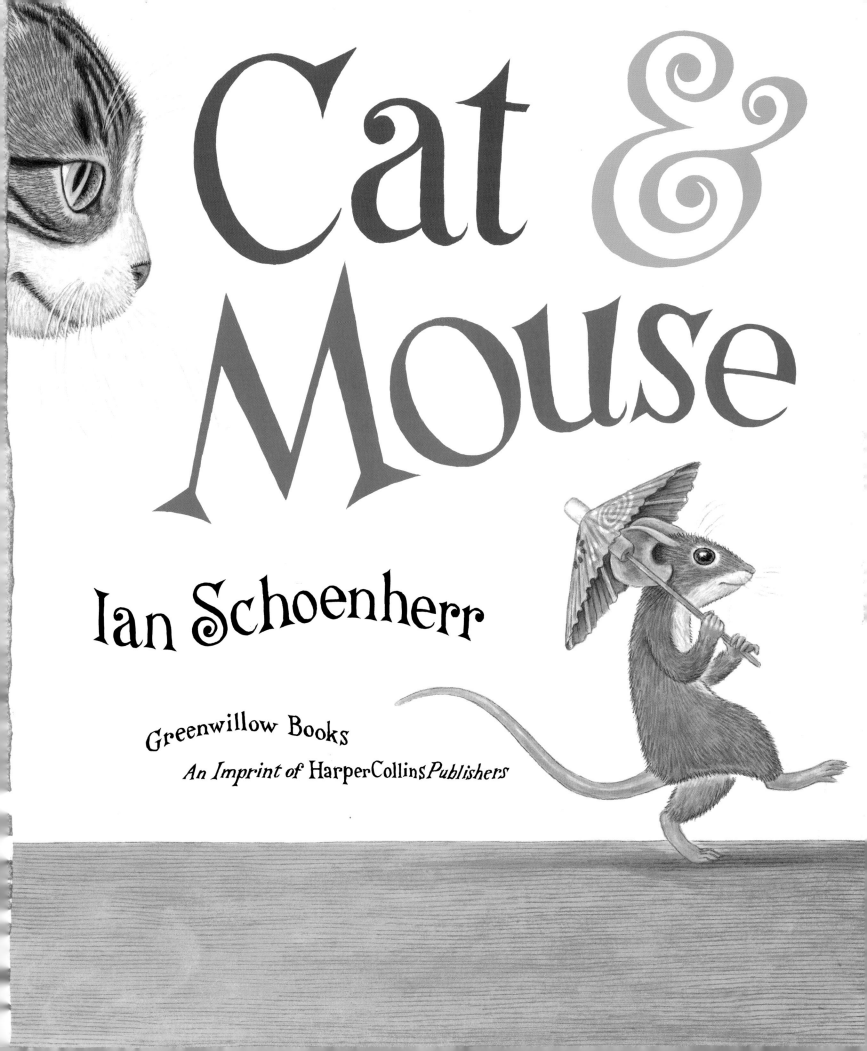

Cat & Mouse

Ian Schoenherr

Greenwillow Books

An Imprint of HarperCollins Publishers

I love little Kitty,
Her coat is so warm.
And if I don't hurt her
She'll do me no harm.

So I won't pull her tail
Nor drive her away,
But Kitty and I
Very gently will play...

Hickory,
dickory,

The mouse ran up

the clock!

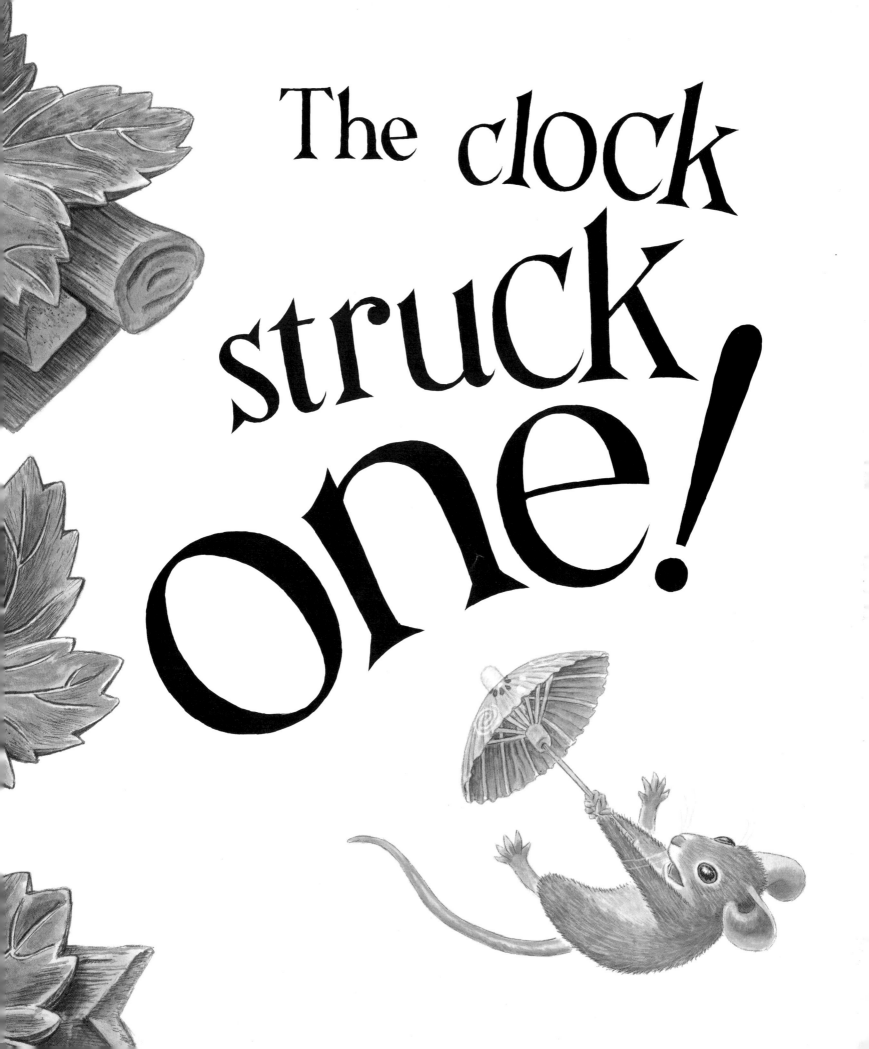

The clock struck one!

The mouse
fell down....

Hickory,

dickory, dock!

I won't pinch her ears
Nor tread on her paw
Lest I provoke her
To use her sharp claw.

I'll never vex her
Nor make her displeased,
For Kitty can't bear
To be worried or teased.

Eeny,
meeny,
miney,
mo?

Catch a

tiger

by the

If she

hollers,

let her

Eeny, meeny, miney, mo!

I'll pat little Kitty
And then she will purr,
And thus show her thanks
For my kindness to her.

She'll sit by my side
And I'll give her some food.
And Kitty will love me
Because I am good.

To my nephews, Sam and Rivers, and to my still-little friends
Coco, Veronica, Mattias, Sam, Blake, Fredricka, and John ~ IS

For the text of this book, I freely adapted three nursery rhymes: "Hickory, Dickory, Dock" and "Eeny, Meeny, Miney, Mo," both of indeterminate age and origin, and "I Love Little Pussy," attributed to the English poet Jane Taylor (1783–1824). She is best known for writing the words to the song "Twinkle, Twinkle, Little Star." The patterns and personalities of my own cats, Buzz and Pistachio, helped me with the pictures, which I made with ink and acrylic paint on watercolor paper.

Cat & Mouse. Copyright © 2008 by Ian Schoenherr. All rights reserved. Manufactured in China. www.harpercollinschildrens.com. Permanent ink and acrylic paint on watercolor paper were used to prepare the full-color art. The text type is hand lettered. Library of Congress Cataloging-in-Publication Data. Schoenherr, Ian. Cat & mouse / by Ian Schoenherr. p. cm. "Greenwillow Books." Summary: A cat and a mouse play together nicely—and not so nicely—to the nursery rhymes "Hickory, Dickory, Dock" and "Eeny, Meeny, Miney, Mo." ISBN 978-0-06-136313-9 (trade bdg.) ISBN 978-0-06-136314-6 (lib. bdg.) [1. Mice—Fiction. 2. Cats—Fiction. 3. Play—Fiction. 4. Nursery rhymes—Fiction. 5. Stories in rhyme.] I. Title. II. Title: Cat and mouse. PZ8.3.S3695Cat 2008 [E]—dc22 2007036145 First Edition 10 9 8 7 6 5 4 3 2 1

Greenwillow Books